This book belongs to

_____

# Cake Mountain

Published by Advance Publishers
www.advance-publishers.com

Written by Ronald Kidd
Illustrated by Dean Kleven, Brad McMahon, and Yakovetic
Editorial development and management by Bumpy Slide Books
Illustrations produced by Disney Publishing Creative Development
Cover design by Deborah Boone

ISBN: 1-57973-022-1

Across from Ant Island, a family was having a
picnic on top of a hill. When they packed up to go
home, they left behind one thing. It was a cupcake.

A bird picked up the cupcake, but found it too large to carry. She dropped it at the edge of Ant Island. Within hours, ant scouts discovered it.

The ant scouts raced back to the anthill and reported their discovery to the Queen. They said they had found a mountain of cake that was big enough to feed the colony for weeks. But they couldn't figure out how to move it.

The Queen asked Thorny, her chief engineer, to come up with a plan.

"I'll do my best," Thorny declared, and he immediately set to work.

The next day, Thorny presented a map to the other ants. The map showed an easy path for the ants to use to get to the mysterious cake mountain.

Then the Queen spoke up. "My, that looks lovely," she said. "But we still don't know how to get the cake *back* to the colony."

The Queen told Thorny to give it more thought and report to her the next day.

Meanwhile, rumors of the cake mountain reached Flik and the other ants.

"I heard that it fell out of the sky," said Dot. "They say it has weird pink goop on top!" exclaimed the Blueberries. "Hey, maybe we can slide on it like this!"

Flik said, "There's only one way to find out. Let's go see for ourselves!"

"Do you think we can?" asked Dot. "It's a long way from here."

Flik just grinned. "We can do it," he said. "It'll be great! You'll see."

The next day, they set out toward the other side of Ant Island. It was a hard journey, but by early afternoon they found what they'd been looking for—the mysterious mound of cake.

"It's gigantic . . . and it tastes good, too!" said Flik, taking a nibble.

Dot scrambled up the side, shouting, "Last one to the top is a stinkbug!"

Everyone climbed up after her—except Flik. He stayed behind and thought and thought.

A few minutes later he called to the others, "Hey, everybody, how would you like to move the cake to the anthill?"

When they asked how, Flik grinned. "We're going to build the world's first cake launcher!"

The other ants laughed. Flik was always having crazy ideas. But he was a nice enough fellow. They decided they would help him out for a little while.

Flik showed the other ants how to slide one end of a stick under the cake mountain. The other end of the stick stuck out over a big rock.

Flik said, "When we're finished, the stick should
work like a giant seesaw. It'll fly the cake all the
way to Ant Island!"

As they worked, a voice called out behind them. "What do you think you're doing?"

It was Thorny, who was still trying to find a last-minute solution of his own.

When Flik explained his plan, Thorny rolled his eyes. "First of all, *I'm* the chief engineer around here. And second, it's obvious this is just another one of your harebrained ideas."

"It'll work! I know it will!" said Flik. "Just give me a chance!"

Sighing, Thorny agreed.

Flik had the other ants collect the biggest rocks they could find, then drop them on the end of the seesaw stick. Nothing happened. They tried again and again, but the cake mountain wouldn't budge.

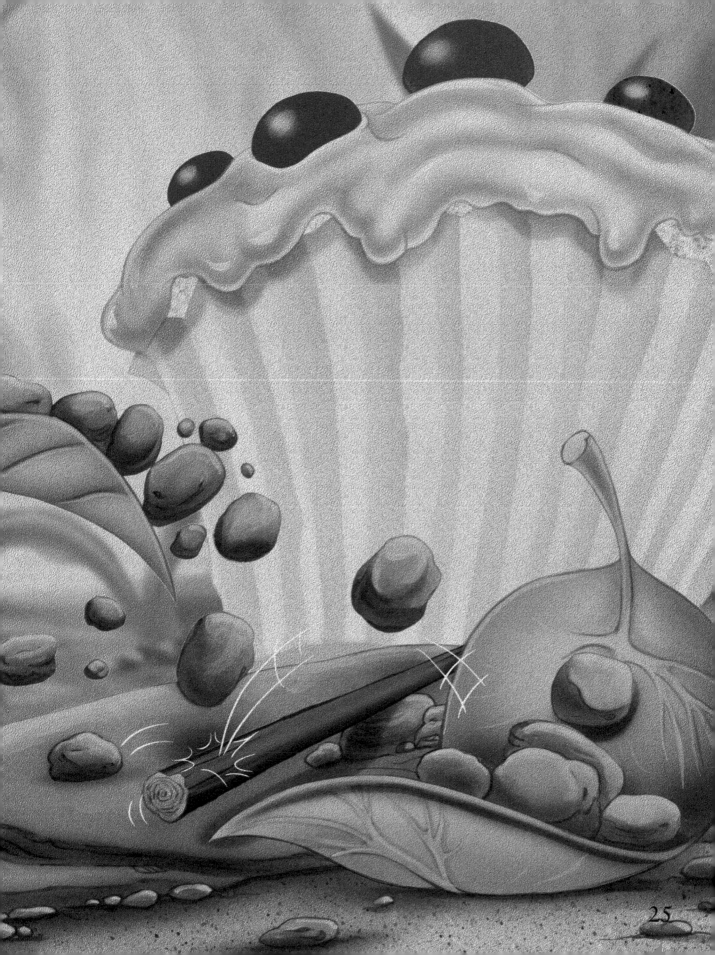

"Of course it won't budge!" snorted Thorny. "To make it work, you'd need something as heavy as the cake mountain on the other end of the seesaw stick. But ants can't move something that heavy."

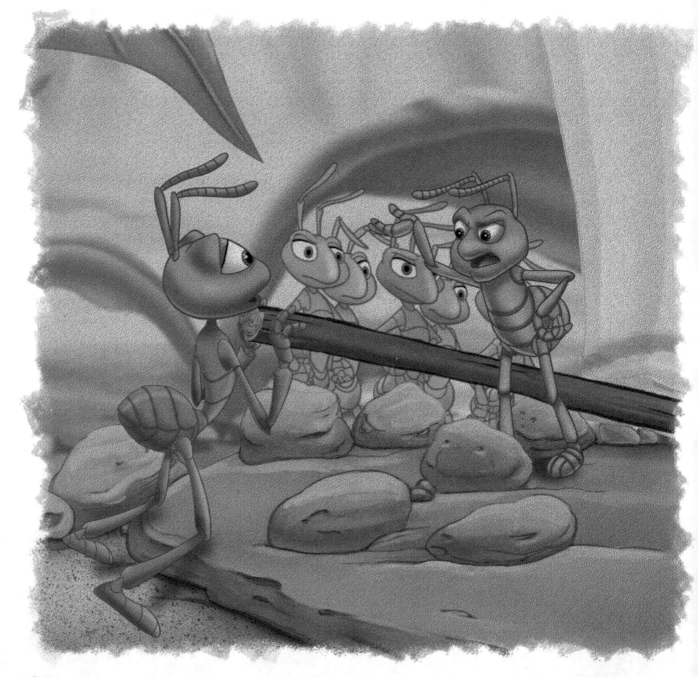

Thorny ordered Flik and the other ants back to the anthill. Then, chuckling at their foolishness, he climbed on top of the cake mountain to take some measurements.

As the other ants headed home, Flik stayed behind to try to figure out another way to fly the cake to the anthill. Suddenly he had an idea. He ran after the other ants and asked some of the stronger ones to come back and help him.

Together, the ants were able to bend a small tree and tie it to the ground with strips of grass. Then Flik told them to roll the cake mountain on top.

By the time they were finished, the ants were so tired that they headed back home to the anthill.

Flik stayed behind to try out his new invention. He didn't know that Thorny was still on top of the cake mountain. When Flik cut the grass strips, the tree snapped up. Thorny hung on for dear life as the cake mountain flew into the air!

Back at the anthill, the Ant Council was beginning to wonder why Thorny had not yet returned from his trip to the cake mountain. Suddenly the sky went dark.

Several ants looked up and saw a giant object
flying through the air, coming straight toward them.
It was the cake mountain!

"Run!" yelled Mr. Soil.

The Council members dove for cover, and the cake mountain landed with a *SPLAT!* Ants came hurrying from everywhere to see what had happened.

Finally, Thorny crawled out from under the mess.
As he brushed himself off, the other members of
the Council applauded.

Mr. Soil shook Thorny's hand. "Congratulations! I didn't doubt you for a moment."

Thorny was very confused. A minute ago, he had been all the way on the other side of Ant Island.

"We don't know how you did it," said the Queen, "but you sure made that cake fly!"

The problem was that Thorny didn't know how it had happened either.

Meanwhile, Flik had run all the way back to the anthill.

"The cake launcher worked!" he told the other ants breathlessly. But none of the other ants was interested in listening to Flik. They were all much too excited by what Thorny had to say.

It seems that the story of the flying cake had already grown into a legend, with Thorny as the hero.

And Flik? The other ants still thought he was just a little ant with big ideas whose gadgets never worked.

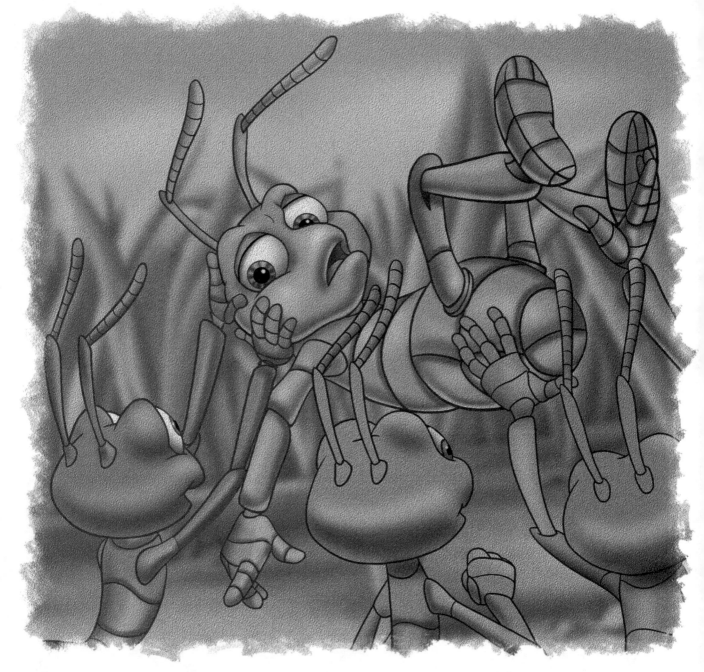

The ants laughed at him, but that didn't bother Flik. He was too excited about the cake launcher, and he hurried off to plan new ways to use it.

Over the days and weeks that followed, Flik came up with dozens of new inventions. Most of them backfired, but that didn't stop Flik from trying. He felt sure that someday, just as he had always dreamed, he would be a hero, too.

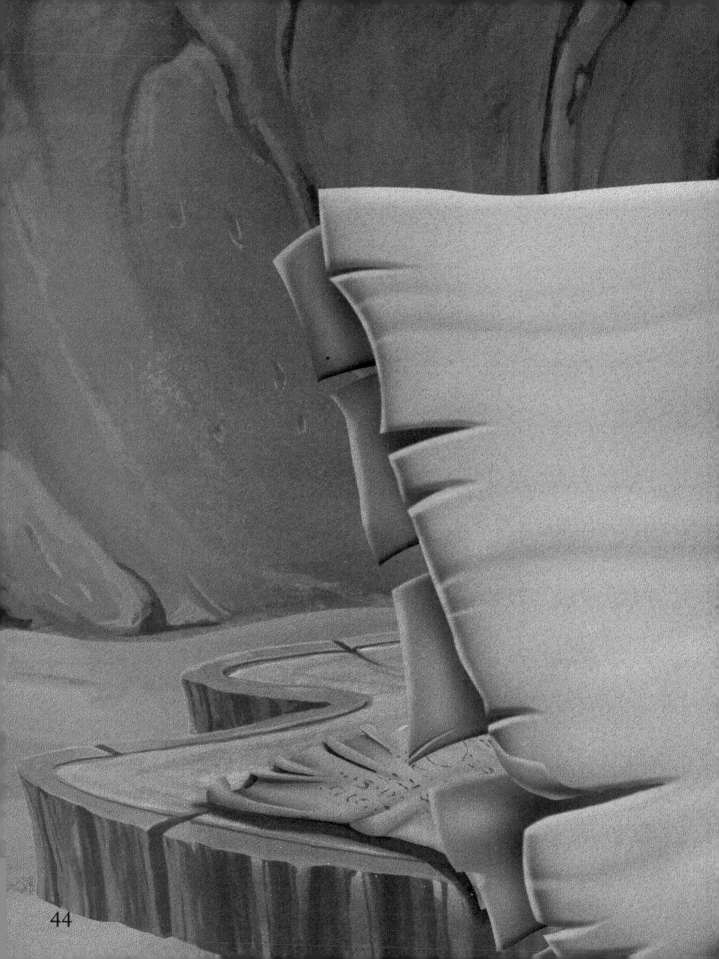

44

Dear Blueberry Journal,

Ants may be little, but we're strong!

Worker ants go out looking for food to bring back to the nest. Sometimes what they find is big.

I've seen them carry huge leaves and giant twigs. Flik says they can carry things that weigh up to 50 times more than they do!

Sometimes they find something really big, like the cake mountain. Then they use their brains instead of their muscles— they break the food into smaller pieces and carry them away. Neat!

Till next time,
Dot